Celebrate Hanukkah with Me

WRITTEN BY *Shari Faden Donahue* PAINTINGS BY *Monica Saurman*

ARIMAX, INC. · WASHINGTON CROSSING, PENNSYLVANIA

This book is dedicated to:

My husband, Tom…My love

My daughters, Maxime and Ariele…My inspiration

My sister, Shelley…My hope

My *Yiddishe mama*, Bec…My encouragement

— S.F.D.

I would like to thank

my mother, Barbara, and my father, Fred,

for their love and guidance…

and for a memorable childhood

filled with tradition and good times.

Special thanks to my husband, Bob,

for his inspiration, support,

and encouragement to pursue life.

— M.V.S.

FOREWORD

As an intermarried Jewish woman living in the Philadelphia suburbs of Bucks County, Pennsylvania, I have placed great emphasis on keeping Judaism alive for our two daughters, Maxime and Ariele, aged thirteen and nine. My husband, Tom, who is Christian, continues to support our Jewish way of life with such pride and enthusiasm that the three of us affectionately refer to him as our "favorite Jewish helper."

My daughters are among a tiny handful of Jewish children at school; they are the only Jewish children at some of their extra-curricular activities. This is especially evident at holiday time when almost everyone in our community celebrates Christmas and Easter, except for us!

My children and I have enjoyed learning about Christianity through the eyes of our non-Jewish neighbors, friends, and extended family. Likewise, I feel it is our responsibility to instill a basic understanding and respect for the great traditions of Judaism, a culture which dates back almost 4,000 years. With this objective in mind, I have written *Celebrate Hanukkah with Me*.

Living as a minority among dominant cultures is a common theme in Jewish history. The story of Hanukkah is especially relevant. In Israel, nearly 200 years prior to the birth of Christ, Jews living under the rule of the Greco-Syrian king, Antiochus, were dominated by the overwhelming presence of Greek culture. Vast numbers of innocent Jewish people were massacred for practicing their most sacred traditions, such as observing the Sabbath, performing the rite of circumcision, and refusing to worship pagan gods.

Many Jews, however, embraced the path of least resistance by assimilating into Greek culture. Enthralled by the modernity of Hellenism, including its nouveau architecture, arts, sports and fashions, they willingly lost sight of their own cherished culture and traditions. Unknowingly, these Jewish Hellenists aided King Antiochus in his mad objective to obliterate Judaism, at any cost.

Thankfully, a small group of Jewish villagers called the Maccabees relentlessly fought against King Antiochus' fierce army, and ultimately won religious freedom. For the past two thousand years, the heroism of the Maccabees has helped to keep Judaism alive in the hearts of Jewish children and adults around the world. With each and every Hanukkah celebration, from generation to generation, the message is strong and unwavering: individuals shall not be "judged" as good or bad, right or wrong, respectable or unworthy, based on their race, religion, or ethnicity.

When living in a community as a minority and feeling "different," a child must be encouraged by parents and teachers alike to joyfully share the wonders and uniqueness of his or her heritage. My hope is to enlighten young readers of all faiths and backgrounds with the knowledge that differences among people are truly non-threatening when addressed with openness, sensitivity, and deeper understanding.

"Guess what, Charlotte,
    it's Hanukkah tonight.

You'll love my brand new dreidels;
    they're so colorful and bright.

I know you've never celebrated
    Hanukkah before.

I'll tell you all about it because
    it's something I adore!"

"Holidays are extra-special when
    I share them with you.

We have so much fun together,
    no matter what we do.

I enjoyed your lovely Christmas party;
    it was as festive as could be.

Now I can't wait for you to celebrate
    the joys of Hanukkah with me!"

"Hanukkah is known as the
    Festival of Lights.

It is religious freedom that I celebrate
    for eight exciting nights.

This is my Menorah;
    it holds nine candles straight.

The Shamesh, the center candle,
    helps me light the other eight."

"By the fourth night, I want more…
But all I light are four!"

"On the third night, wait and see…
I won't light more than three!"

"On the second night, it's true…
I adore lighting two!"

"On the first night, I have fun…
Just lighting candle one!"

"When the fifth night does arrive…
I am eager to light five!"

"The sixth night is a treat…
Because lighting six is neat!"

"The seventh night's amazing…
Watching seven flames ablazing!"

"And the final night's so great…
Because I get to light all eight!"

"As I light the Hanukkah candles
for eight nights in a row,

I proudly remember the Maccabees
who lived so long ago.

These heroes fought for religious
freedom, and won–
I'm relieved!

With courage, they stood
strongly for what
they believed."

"The Jewish Maccabees led my ancestors against Antiochus, the Syrian king–

Who commanded them to worship every idol his evil army could bring."

"My ancestors would not
bow down to statues,
and therefore disobeyed.

They believed in one God, as I do,
and were killed as they prayed.

Charlotte, if I lived back then,
I would have been so afraid!"

"The brave Maccabees were small in number,
    but struck secretly at night.

"The Maccabees reclaimed the Holy Temple and tossed the idols away.

They found a tiny jug of oil to light the Menorah for only one day."

"A miracle did happen…the oil continued to blaze.
The sacred light of the Menorah lasted eight entire days!"

"Eight days of miraculous light–
so incredible, you see…

The shining light of freedom
still glows inside of me!"

"I love celebrating Hanukkah
   with friends and family every night.

Thank goodness those brave Maccabees
   won that freedom fight!"

"I can't wait for you to come to my house just as soon as school is done.

We'll eat special pancakes called latkes, spin dreidels, and have so much fun!"

"Though our religions may be different,
great friends we'll forever be–

Because I love to learn about you...
and you love to learn about me!"

With pride,

I honor the memory of:

My father, Leon Leigh Faden,

My bubbie, Dora Balter,

And the mother-in-law I wish I could have known,

Charlotte McKinney Donahue,

Whose name lives in the pages of this book.

— S.F.D.

ARIMAX, INC.
Post Office Box 53
Washington Crossing, Pennsylvania 18977
Phone: (215) 862-5899
Fax: (215) 862-9720
E-mail: Arimax1@aol.com

Editor: Rochelle (Shelley) Faden
Rabbinical Consultant: Rabbi Yehuda Shemtov
Library of Congress Catalog Card Number: 98-93674
ISBN: 0-9634287-2-1